HERBIE'S TROUBLES

by Carol Chapman
illustrated by Kelly Oechsli

E. P. Dutton   New York

Library of Congress Cataloging in Publication Data

Chapman, Carol.   Herbie's troubles.

Summary: Herbie's attitude toward school quickly
changes the day he meets Jimmy John.
[1. Bullies—Fiction.   2. School stories]
I. Oechsli, Kelly.   II. Title.
PZ7.C36636He   1981   [E]   80-21848
ISBN 0-525-31645-0

Published in the United States by Elsevier-Dutton
Publishing Co., Inc., 2 Park Avenue, New York, N.Y. 10016

Published simultaneously in Canada by Clarke,
Irwin & Company Limited, Toronto and Vancouver

Editor: Ann Durell   Designer: Susan Lu

Printed in the U.S.A.   First Edition
10 9 8 7 6 5 4 3 2

to Ann Durell:
my fairy godmother in the East

Herbie was six and one-half. He liked his mom, his dad, the kids on his block, most vegetables, and his baby sister.

Herbie also liked school. But that quickly changed the day he met Jimmy John.

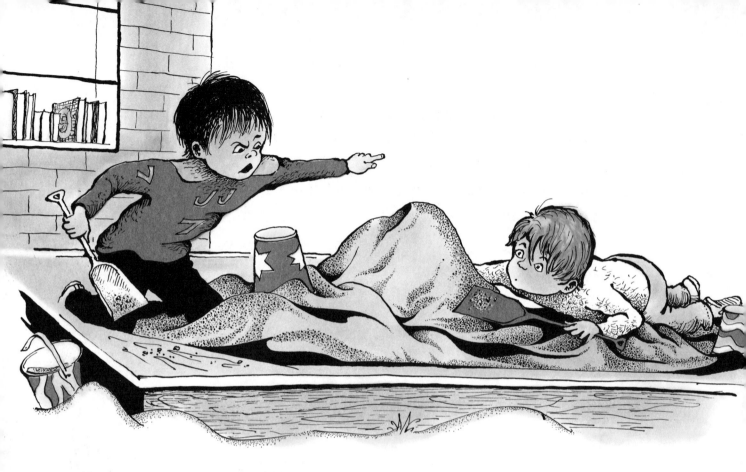

Jimmy John was in the sandbox making a tunnel.
Herbie was in the sandbox making a tunnel too. Then
their two tunnels met.

Jimmy John squinted at Herbie. "Your tunnel is in
my tunnel's way. Move it!"

"How can I move it?" asked Herbie.

"Like this!" said Jimmy John. And he dumped Herbie's tunnel right into Herbie's lap.

That was only the beginning of Herbie's troubles.

The next day when Herbie was painting a picture of
a dinosaur, Jimmy John said, "That dinosaur is dumb!"
Jimmy John then splattered paint all over Herbie's
dinosaur.

The following Monday, Jimmy John swiped Herbie's granola bar and smashed it.

On Tuesday, Jimmy John tied Herbie's jacket sleeves into a knot.

And on Friday, Jimmy John held the door shut so
Herbie couldn't get out.

Life at school kept getting worse and worse for Herbie. He didn't play in the sandbox anymore. He didn't dare eat his granola bars. And he had to make double sure he didn't go into the bathroom when Jimmy John did.

As a matter of fact, it got to the point that Herbie didn't even like going to school anymore.

One morning he decided he just was not going!

"Aren't you going to school?" asked Sophie, who lived in the third house from the end.

"Nope," said Herbie. Then he told Sophie about all the rotten things that Jimmy John did to him.

"I think," said Sophie, "you should just tell Jimmy John that you don't like what he does to you. Nowadays people have to be assertive!"

"Will that work?" asked Herbie.

"Yep!" said Sophie. "I do it all the time."

So Herbie marched off to school. And that very morning he walked right up to Jimmy John.

"I don't want you to bother me anymore!"

"How come?" asked Jimmy John.

"Because I don't like it!" answered Herbie.

"Good," said Jimmy John, pulling a button off Herbie's sweater.

The next day Herbie was most definitely
not going to school!

"Aren't you going to school?" asked Mary Ellen, who lived in the house across the street.

"Nope!" said Herbie. And he told Mary Ellen about all the rotten things that Jimmy John did to him.

"I think," said Mary Ellen, twirling a curl, "you should share a treat with Jimmy John."

"Will that work?" asked Herbie.

"Yes," said Mary Ellen. "I do it all the time."

So Herbie marched off to school. And at lunchtime
he carefully split his slice of chocolate cake in half.

"Here," said Herbie. "Have a piece of cake."

"I hate chocolate cake!"

Unfortunately, Herbie was wearing his favorite shirt
that day!

The next day Herbie was most definitely, for sure, not going to school!

"Aren't you going to school?" asked Jake, who lived in the house around the corner.

"Nope," said Herbie. And he told Jake about all the rotten things that Jimmy John did to him.

"I think," said Jake, as he chomped on gum, "you should punch Jimmy John right in the nose."

"Will that work?" asked Herbie.

"And how!" said Jake. "I do it all the time."

So Herbie marched off to school. And the minute he saw
Jimmy John, he punched him right in the nose. Jimmy
John punched Herbie right in the stomach.

They both got sent to the office.

The next day Herbie was most definitely, for sure, without a doubt, not going to school.

And he wasn't going to take any more advice either. Because obviously, what worked for Sophie, Mary Ellen and Jake did not work for him!

So there Herbie sat, knowing he'd never, ever go to
school again. Even though, sighed Herbie, that meant
he'd never find out what came after P in the alphabet.
And he'd never see if his lima bean sprouted. And—oh
no! He'd miss out on the trip to the hog farm!

At that last thought, Herbie suddenly got up. He squared his jaw. There were times in a kid's life when he had to take matters into his own hands. And now was the time. There was just too much at stake.

It was going to be hard! It was going to be tough! But, he had to do what he had to do!

And that very day, when Jimmy John splattered paint
on Herbie's picture—Herbie just kept on painting.

When Jimmy John stepped on Herbie's tunnel—
Herbie made another tunnel.

When Jimmy John swiped Herbie's granola bar—
Herbie ate his apple instead.

And when Jimmy John held the door shut—
Herbie just crawled under it.

As Herbie started to walk away, he heard Jimmy John
mumble, "Aaaah, you're no fun anymore!"

And now Herbie is six and one-half and two weeks. He likes his mom, his dad, the kids on his block, most vegetables, his baby sister, and once again—school!

check check
check